A Bilingual Anthology
of Classic Fairy Tales

Aprende inglés
con los cuentos de siempre

© 2013. Adaptation & Translation | Adaptación y traducción
Stacy & Chuck Wrinkle

© 2013. Illustrations | Ilustraciones
Javier Muñoz

© 2013. Bilingual Readers
Pza. Mostenses, 13 - of. 26
28015 Madrid
91 758 06 06
bilingualreaders.com | bilingualreaders.es
facebook.com/bilingualreaders | twitter.com/BilingualRdrs

First Edition | Primera edición
March 2013 | Marzo de 2013

Printed in China | Impreso en China

ISBN: 978-84-92968-25-1

M-38263-2012

Printed by | Impreso por
Leo Paper

A Bilingual Anthology of Classic Fairy Tales

Aprende inglés con los cuentos de siempre

Illustrations | Ilustraciones
Javier Muñoz

BILINGUAL
READERS

Table of Contents | Índice

Introduction | Introducción ... 9

Tales | Cuentos

Vocabulary & Activities | Vocabulario y ejercicios
www.bilingualreaders.com | www.bilingualreaders.es

Introduction

In this new volume of the collection Cuentos del Mundo, we present you with a selection of twenty-five adapted versions of classic fairy tales. Just like in the previous books in this collection, each bilingual story includes highlighted vocabulary words. On our website you will also find a series of activities and exercises with their corresponding solutions.

We hope our readers will treasure this new volume as much as they have the other books in this collection. And if, in addition to enjoying these wonderful classic fairy tales, readers also have fun learning languages, we will have accomplished our goal.

Introducción

En este nuevo volumen de la colección Cuentos del Mundo presentamos una selección adaptada de veinticinco cuentos tradicionales. Como en las obras precedentes, en cada cuento se han resaltado palabras de vocabulario, y en nuestra web proponemos una serie de actividades y ejercicios con sus soluciones correspondientes.

Confiamos en que esta nueva selección sea tan bien acogida como los otros libros de la colección. Si además de disfrutar con estos maravillosos cuentos tradicionales nos divertimos y aprendemos idiomas, habremos conseguido nuestro objetivo.

GOLDILOCKS AND THE THREE BEARS

There was once a pretty little girl named Goldilocks who lived near a forest. One day she grew **tired of** playing with her toys and wandered off into the woods. She came upon a funny little house, which belonged to a family of bears. But when Goldilocks entered the house, she found no one at home since Papa Bear, Mama Bear and Baby Bear had all **gone out for a walk** while their dinner was cooling. When Goldilocks **smelled** the wonderful soup, **she couldn't resist** taking just one small sip from Papa Bear's bowl. "It's too hot!" she cried when she had tasted it. "This one is **too** cold!" she complained when she tried Mama Bear's soup. "This one is **just right!**" she exclaimed when she tried Baby Bear's soup, and she was so hungry that she ate it all. Then Goldilocks was very tired so she went upstairs to find a place to lie down for a nap. She tried Papa Bear's bed, but it was too hard. Mama Bear's bed was quickly found to be too soft. But Baby Bear's bed felt just right, and Goldilocks fell fast asleep. When the Bear family came home, they immediately knew that someone had been in their house. "Someone **tasted** my soup!" cried Papa Bear. "Someone tasted mine, too!" complained Mama Bear. "Someone tasted my soup and ate it all up!" cried Baby Bear while tears fell down his cheeks. The Bear family quickly marched up the **stairs** to see if their intruder was still in the house. When Goldilocks awoke to see the three bears looking down at her, she was so scared that she jumped out the window! She ran all the way home and into her mother's arms, and she never went near the Bear family's house again.

RICITOS DE ORO Y LOS TRES OSOS

Había una vez una preciosa niñita llamada Ricitos de Oro que vivía junto a un bosque. **Aburrida de** sus juguetes, un día Ricitos de Oro se adentró en el bosque y, al rato, se topó con una pequeña casita que pertenecía a una familia de osos. Ricitos de Oro entró en la casa, pero la encontró vacía, puesto que Papá Oso, Mamá Osa y el Osito habían **salido a dar un paseo** mientras se enfriaba la cena. Cuando Ricitos de Oro **olió** la riquísima sopa, **no pudo resistirse** a dar un sorbito del plato de Papá Oso. «¡Cómo quema!», gritó después de probarla. «Esta está **demasiado** fría», se quejó al probar la sopa de Mamá Osa. «¡Esta está **en su punto!**», exclamó al probar la sopa del Osito, y estaba tan hambrienta que se la tomó entera. Ricitos se sentía muy cansada, así que subió al primer piso para encontrar un sitio en el que echarse a dormir una siesta. Probó la cama de Papá Oso, pero era demasiado dura. La cama de Mamá Osa fue descartada rápidamente por ser demasiado blanda. Sin embargo, la cama del Osito era perfecta, y Ricitos de Oro se quedó dormida enseguida. Cuando la familia Oso regresó a casa, notó de inmediato que alguien había estado allí. «¡Alguien **ha probado** mi sopa!», exclamó Papá Oso. «¡También la mía!», añadió Mamá Osa. «¡Alguien ha probado mi sopa y se la ha comido toda!», sollozó el Osito con lágrimas en las mejillas. Rápidamente la familia Oso subió las **escaleras** para comprobar si el intruso aún estaba en casa. Cuando Ricitos de Oro despertó y se encontró con que tres osos la miraban, se asustó tanto que ¡saltó por la ventana! Corrió hasta llegar a casa y encontrarse en brazos de su madre, y nunca volvió a acercarse a la casa de la familia Oso.

THE THREE BROTHERS

An old man had three sons, but no fortune except the house he lived in. Each of the brothers wanted **to inherit** the house after his death, but their father did not know how **to treat them all fairly**. At last he had an idea. "Go out into the world and learn a **trade**," he said. "When you come home, the one who makes the best use of his trade will get the house." The three brothers all found masters, and each learned his trade very well. One became a well known **barber**, who only cut the hair of the richest men in town. Another became a famous **baker** who only baked for the royal family. The third became a swordsmith and made swords for the highest ranking members of the royal **army**. When they all came home to show off their new talents, their father was astonished at how well his sons had done. But he was most impressed by the swordsmith, who used his sword so well in the rain that his blade kept both himself and his family dry during a **storm**. But his brothers **did not complain** when their father gave him the house since the brothers all loved each other very much. The swordsmith invited his brothers to stay in the house with him, and there they all lived happily ever after.

LOS TRES HERMANOS

Un hombre ya mayor tenía tres hijos, y ninguna propiedad excepto la casa en la que vivía. Todos querían **heredar** la casa tras su muerte, pero el padre no sabía cómo **ser justo con todos ellos**. Por fin, tuvo una idea. «Salid a recorrer mundo y aprended un **oficio** –les dijo–. Cuando regreséis, el que mejor se desenvuelva se quedará con la casa». Los tres hermanos tuvieron buenos maestros y aprendieron su oficio muy bien. Uno se convirtió en un afamado **barbero** que solo cortaba el pelo de los más ricos del pueblo. Otro llegó a ser un prestigioso **panadero** que solo horneaba para la familia real. El tercero se convirtió en espadero y fabricaba espadas para los más altos mandos del **ejército** real. Cuando volvieron a casa para mostrar sus habilidades, su padre quedó maravillado de lo bien que lo habían hecho sus hijos. Sin embargo, quien más lo impresionó fue el espadero, que usaba la espada tan bien que la hoja podía mantenerlo seco a él y a su familia bajo la lluvia de una **tormenta**. De modo que sus hermanos **no se quejaron** cuando su padre le hizo heredero de la casa, pues todos los hermanos se querían mucho. El espadero invitó a sus hermanos a quedarse en la casa con él, y allí vivieron todos felices para siempre.

THE WREN AND THE BEAR

One summer's day the bear and the wolf were walking together when they heard the sweet song of a bird. "What kind of bird is that who sings so beautifully?" asked the bear. "That is the king of the birds," explained the wolf, though it was really just an ordinary wren. The bear begged the wolf to take him to the royal palace. The wolf led him to the wren's **nest**, but **he warned** the bear to wait until the king and queen were gone before he looked inside. When the king and queen had left, the bear looked into the nest and was shocked to see five or six very ordinary looking baby birds. "Is this the royal palace? You don't look like little princes at all!" the bear exclaimed and walked away. "We are little princes, and you will pay for what you have said!" the birds shouted in reply. When the king and queen returned, the baby birds **refused to eat** because they were so insulted by what the bear had said. The wrens were then left with no choice but to **declare war on** the bear. They gathered up an army of all the flying things in the forest, including all kinds of birds, **bees, wasps** and other flying insects. Meanwhile, the bear was busy recruiting his army of all the four- legged creatures in the forest. When the four-legged animals were planning their strategy, the wrens sent a tiny gnat as a **spy** to listen to their plans. When the four- legged animals had decided that the fox would hold up his tail as a signal that the rest of the army should follow him into battle, the gnat quickly flew away to tell the king and queen. When the fox marched into battle, the wasps immediately began to sting his tail until he could not hold it up straight. The rest of his army was afraid and ran away to their homes. Finally, the bear was forced **to apologize** to the little wrens so that peace could be restored in the forest.

EL REYEZUELO Y EL OSO

Un día de verano caminaban juntos un oso y un lobo cuando oyeron la dulce canción de un pájaro. «¿Qué clase de pájaro canta tan hermosamente?», preguntó el oso. «Es el rey de los pájaros», le contestó el lobo, aunque en realidad era un reyezuelo normal y corriente. El oso le suplicó al lobo que lo llevara al palacio real. El lobo lo condujo hasta el **nido** del reyezuelo, pero **le advirtió** al oso que esperara hasta que el rey y la reina se hubieran marchado antes de mirar dentro. Cuando el rey y la reina se hubieron marchado, el oso miró el interior del nido, y se sorprendió al ver cinco o seis pajarillos de aspecto corriente. «¿Este es el palacio real? ¡No parecéis principitos en absoluto!», exclamó el oso, y se alejó. «¡Somos principitos, y pagarás por lo que has dicho!», replicaron los pájaros. Cuando el rey y la reina regresaron, los pajaritos **se negaron a comer** por lo insultados que se sentían por las palabras del oso. Los reyezuelos no tuvieron más remedio que **declararle la guerra al** oso. Reunieron un ejército de todo tipo de animales voladores del bosque que incluía pájaros, **abejas, avispas** y otros insectos voladores. Mientras tanto, el oso se encontraba ocupado reclutando en el bosque un ejército de criaturas de cuatro patas. Cuando los animales de cuatro patas preparaban su estrategia, los reyezuelos enviaron a un minúsculo mosquito como **espía** para que escuchara sus planes. Cuando los animales de cuatro patas habían decidido que el zorro mantendría su cola recta como señal de que el resto del ejército debía seguirlo a la batalla, el mosquito rápidamente volvió para contárselo al rey y a la reina. Cuando el zorro entró en combate, de inmediato las avispas comenzaron a picarle en la cola, hasta que no pudo sostenerla recta. El resto del ejército se asustó y regresó corriendo a casa. Finalmente, el oso tuvo que **disculparse** ante los pequeños reyezuelos, para que la paz pudiera volver al bosque.

THE FOX AND THE CAT

One fine day the cat met Mr. Fox in the woods, and because she thought he was **clever** and experienced in all the ways of the world, she spoke to him in a friendly manner. "Good-morning, dear Mr. Fox! How are you, and how are you doing in these **hard times**?" The fox, full of **pride**, looked at the cat from head to foot for some time, hardly knowing whether he should even answer her or not. At last he said, "Oh, you poor little feline, you silly **housepet**, you sad little mouse hunter! **Who do you think you are?** How dare you ask me how I am doing? What sort of education have you had? How many arts are you master of?" "Only one," said the cat meekly. "And what might that one be?" asked the fox. "When the dogs run after me, I can jump into a tree and save myself." "Is that all?" said the fox. "I am master of a hundred arts, and I have a sackful of cunning tricks. But **I feel sorry for you**. Come with me, and I will teach you how to escape from the dogs." Just then a **hunter** came along with four hounds. The cat immediately jumped into a tree, and crept stealthily to the topmost branch, where she was entirely hidden by twigs and leaves. "**Show me** your tricks, Mr. Fox! Show me your tricks!" cried the cat, but the dogs had caught him firmly and wouldn't let him go. "Oh, Mr. Fox!" cried the cat, "with your hundred arts and your sackful of tricks, you have been trapped; while I, with my one small trick, am safe. Why didn't you just **climb the tree** with me?"

EL ZORRO Y LA GATA

Un buen día la gata se encontró con el Señor Zorro en el bosque, y como lo consideraba **astuto** y experimentado en los asuntos de la vida, le habló de manera amigable. «¡Buenos días, Señor Zorro, ¿cómo está, y cómo le va en estos **tiempos difíciles**?». El zorro, lleno de **orgullo**, miró a la gata de arriba abajo durante un tiempo, incapaz de decidir si debía siquiera contestar, o no. Al fin, le dijo: «¡Ah, tú, pobre felino, **mascota** tonta, triste cazarratones! **¿Quién te has creído?** ¿Cómo te atraves a preguntarme cómo estoy? ¿Qué clase de educación te han dado? ¿Cuántas artes dominas?». «Solo una», respondió la gata mansamente. «¿Y de qué se trata?», preguntó el zorro. «Cuando los perros me persiguen, puedo encaramarme a un árbol y salvarme». «¿Eso es todo? –replicó el zorro–. Yo domino cien artes y cuento con un saco lleno de astutos trucos. Pero **te compadezco**. Acompáñame y te mostraré cómo escapar de los perros». Justo entonces un **cazador** llegó hasta allí con cuatro sabuesos. Inmediatamente, la gata saltó a un árbol y se deslizó con sigilo hasta la rama más alta, donde quedó oculta por completo por ramas y hojas. «¡**Enséñeme** sus trucos, Señor Zorro, enséñeme sus trucos!», le gritó la gata, pero los sabuesos lo tenían bien sujeto y no lo dejaron escapar. «¡Oh, Señor Zorro! –gritó la gata–. Con sus cien artes y su saco de trucos, le han atrapado, mientras que yo, con mi única habilidad, estoy a salvo. ¿Por qué no **se subió al árbol** conmigo?».

THE RATS AND THEIR SON-IN-LAW

There once lived in Japan a rat and his wife, who had one beautiful daughter. They were exceedingly proud of her charms and **dreamed of** the grand marriage she was sure to make. Proud of his pure rodent blood, the father saw no **son-in-law** more to be desired than a young rat of ancient lineage, who also appeared to be very much in love with his daughter. This **match**, however, seemed not to the mother's taste. Like many people who think themselves made out of special clay, she had a very poor opinion of her own kind, and she was ambitious for an alliance with the **highest circles**.

Thus she spoke to the sun about marrying their daughter. "Mr. Sun," said the mother, "let me present our only daughter, who is so beautiful that there is nothing like her in the whole world." But the sun replied that she should talk to someone even greater than he, the cloud. **At that very moment** the cloud came and covered up the sun, and the mother wasted no time in addressing him. "I'm honored," said the cloud, "but you should speak to the wind, who is even greater than I." Then the wind blew the rat family over until they stopped at the foot of an old wall. When the mother made her proposal to the wind, he told her to speak to the wall, as it was able to stop the wind. Yet the rat-maiden didn't want to marry the wall, since she much preferred the young rat who had been courting her for some time. **Fortunately**, the wall spoke of the **strength** of the rat, who can easily pass through walls. "**Did you hear that?**" cried father-rat in triumph. "Quite true!" returned the mother-rat in wonder.

So they all three went home, very happy and contented, and the following day the lovely rat-maiden married her faithful rat-lover.

LAS RATAS Y SU YERNO

Había una vez en Japón una rata y su mujer, que tenían una bellísima hija. Estaban muy orgullosos de sus encantos y **soñaban con** la gran boda que la esperaba. Orgulloso de la pureza de su sangre de roedor, el padre no encontró otro roedor más deseable como **yerno** que una joven rata de antiguo linaje, que además también parecía muy enamorado de su hija. Sin embargo, esta **unión** no era del agrado de la madre. Como mucha gente que se cree hecha de una arcilla especial, tenía en baja consideración a los de su clase, y ambicionaba una unión con las **altas esferas**.

Por ello habló con el sol para que se casase con su hija. «Señor Sol –dijo la madre–, permítame presentarle a nuestra única hija, que es tan bella que no hay nada como ella en todo el mundo». Sin embargo, el sol respondió que deberían hablar con alguien incluso más poderoso que él, la nube. **En ese preciso instante** la nube llegó y tapó el sol, y la madre no tardó ni un segundo en dirigirse a él. «Es un honor –replicó la nube–, pero deberíais hablar con el viento, que es incluso mejor que yo». Entonces sopló el viento y arrastró a la familia rata hasta que fueron detenidos por una pared. Cuando la madre hizo la proposición al viento, este le dijo que hablase con la pared, que era capaz de parar el viento. Pero la rata casamentera no quería casarse con la pared, puesto que prefería casarse con la joven rata que la había cortejado durante un tiempo. **Por suerte**, la pared habló de la **fuerza** de la rata, que puede atravesar paredes fácilmente. «**¿Lo has oído?**», exclamó el padre rata triunfal. «¡Cierto!», replicó la rata madre con asombro.

Así que regresaron a casa los tres, muy contentos y satisfechos, y al día siguiente la bella novia rata se casó con su fiel amante.

THE MOUSE AND THE SAUSAGE

Once upon a time a little mouse and a little sausage, who loved each other like sisters, decided to **live together**. They made their arrangements in such a way that every day one would go to walk in the fields or **run errands** in town, while the other remained at home **to keep the house**.

One day, when the little sausage had prepared cabbage for dinner, the little mouse, who had come back from town with a fine appetite, enjoyed it so much that she exclaimed: "How delicious the cabbage is today, my dear!"

"Ah!" answered the little sausage, "that is because I popped myself into the pot while it was cooking."

On the next day, as **it was her turn** to prepare the meal, the little mouse said to herself: "Now I will do as much for my friend as she did for me. We will have lentils for dinner, and **I will jump** into the pot while they are boiling." And so she did, without reflecting that a simple sausage can do some things which are not possible for even the wisest mouse. When the sausage came home, she found the house lonely and silent. She called **again and again**, "My little mouse! Mouse of my heart!" but no one answered. Then she went to look at the lentils boiling on the stove. There in the pot she found her little friend, who had perished at the post of duty.

Poor mousie, **with the best intentions** in the world, had stayed **too long** at her cookery, and when she desired to climb out of the pot, she no longer had the strength to do so.

And the poor sausage could never be consoled! That is why today, when you put a sausage in the pan, you will hear her weep and **sigh**, "M-my p-poor m-mouse! Ah, m-my p-poor m-mouse!"

LA RATONA Y LA SALCHICHA

Había una vez una pequeña ratona y una pequeña salchicha que se querían como hermanas, que decidieron **irse a vivir juntas**. Acordaron que cada día una de ellas iría a pasear por los campos o a **hacer recados** al pueblo, mientras la otra se quedaría **cuidando de la casa**.

Un día que la pequeña salchicha había preparado col para cenar, la pequeña ratona, que había vuelto del pueblo hambrienta, se alegró tanto que exclamó: «¡Querida, hoy esta col está deliciosa!».

«¡Ah! –respondió la pequeña salchicha–, eso es porque me he metido en la olla mientras se cocinaba!».

Al día siguiente, que **le tocaba** preparar la comida, la pequeña ratona se dijo: «Voy a hacer tanto por mi amiga como ella ha hecho por mí. Para cenar tendremos lentejas, y **saltaré** a la olla cuando se estén cocinando». Y así lo hizo, sin pensar que una simple salchicha puede hacer algunas cosas que ni siquiera el más listo de los ratones puede hacer. Cuando la salchicha volvió a casa, la encontró vacía y en silencio. La salchicha gritó **una y otra vez**: «¡Mi pequeña ratona, ratona de mi corazón!», pero nadie respondió. Entonces se acercó a mirar las lentejas que se cocían al fuego. Ahí en la olla encontró a su pequeña amiga, que había perecido en cumplimiento del deber.

Pobre ratona, **con la mejor intención** del mundo había estado **demasiado tiempo** en la cocción, y cuando quiso salir de la olla ya no tuvo fuerza suficiente.

¡Y la pobre salchicha nunca pudo ser consolada! Por eso hoy en día, cuando pones una salchicha en la sartén, puedes oír cómo llora y **suspira**: «¡M-mi p-pequeña ratona! ¡M-mi p-pequeña ratona!».

THE CAMEL AND THE PIG

One day a camel **bragged** to his friends: "**There sure is nothing like** being tall! See how tall I am? Don't you wish you were tall, too?" A pig who heard these words said, "There sure is nothing like being short. Look how short I am! Don't you wish you were short, too?"

The camel said, "Well, I can prove that being tall is better. I'll bet you my **hump** that it's true."

The pig said, "If I fail to prove the truth of what I have said, I will give up my **snout**."

"Agreed!" said the camel.

"Just so!" said the pig.

The two friends soon came to a garden enclosed by a low wall without any opening. The camel stood on the side the wall, and, reaching the plants within by means of his long neck, ate them for breakfast. Then he turned jeeringly to the pig, who had been standing at the bottom of the wall, without even having a look at the good things in the garden, and said, "Now, **would you rather** be tall or short?"

Next they came to a garden enclosed by a high wall, with a small gate at one end. The pig entered by the gate, and, after having eaten his fill of the vegetables within, came out, **laughing at** the poor camel, who had had to stay outside because he was too tall to enter the garden by the gate. "Now," said the pig, "would you rather be tall or short?"

Then the two friends thought the matter over, and **came to the conclusion** that the camel should keep his hump and the pig should keep his snout. The camel and the pig both observed that there were **advantages** to being both tall and short, and they remained good friends for the rest of their days.

EL CAMELLO Y EL CERDO

Un día un camello **se chuleaba** ante sus amigos: «¡**No hay nada mejor que** ser alto! ¿Veis lo alto que soy? ¿No os gustaría ser altos también?». Un cerdo que oyó estas palabras replicó: «No hay nada como ser bajo. ¡Mira qué bajo soy! ¿No os gustaría ser bajos como yo?».

El camello dijo: «Bueno, puedo demostrar que ser alto es mejor. Te apuesto mi **joroba** a que es verdad». El cerdo, por su parte, añadió: «Si no consigo demostrar que lo que he dicho es verdad, renuncio a mi **hocico**».

«¡De acuerdo!», exclamó el camello.

«¡Igualmente!», concedió el cerdo.

Enseguida los dos amigos llegaron hasta un jardín rodeado de una pequeña valla sin ninguna abertura. El camello se quedó junto a la valla y, gracias a su largo cuello, alcanzó las plantas que rodeaban el jardín y se las comió para desayunar. Entonces se giró burlonamente hacia el cerdo, que se había quedado en la parte inferior de la valla, sin siquiera mirar las buenas cosas del jardín, y le dijo: «Y ahora, ¿**preferirías** ser alto o bajo?».

Luego se acercaron a un jardín rodeado por una alta valla, con una pequeña puerta en un extremo. El cerdo atravesó la puerta y, después de haberse comido las plantas de dentro, salió y **se rio del** pobre camello, que se había tenido que quedar fuera, pues era demasiado alto para pasar por la puerta. «Y ahora ―dijo el cerdo―, ¿preferirías ser alto o bajo?».

Entonces ambos amigos pensaron sobre el asunto y **llegaron a la conclusión** de que el camello debía quedarse su joroba, y el cerdo, su hocico. Tanto el camello como el cerdo se dieron cuenta de que había **ventajas** tanto en ser alto como bajo, y siguieron siendo amigos para el resto de sus vidas.

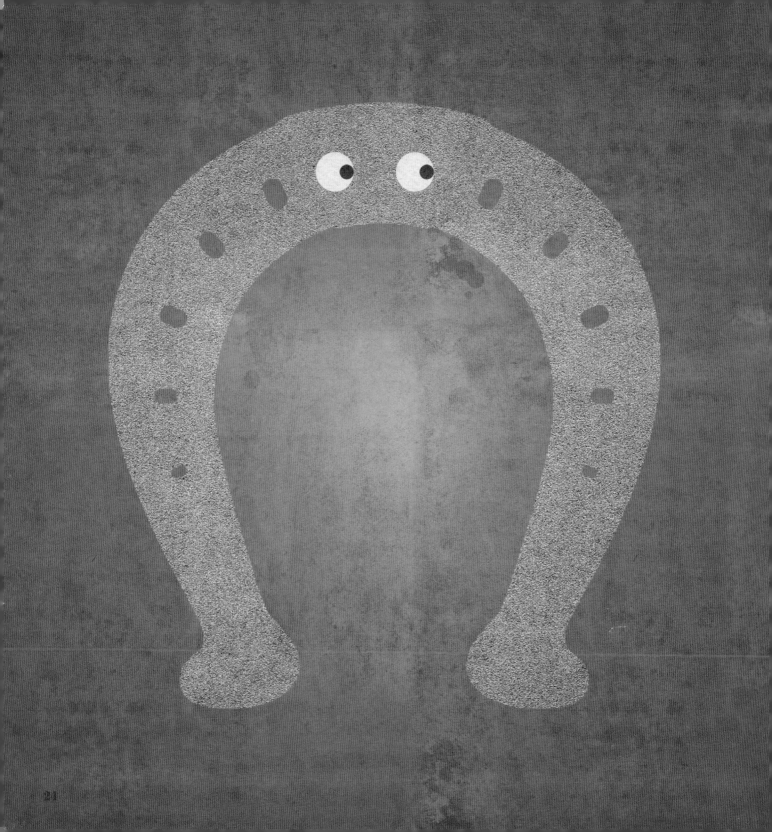

THE NAIL

One day a tradesman had a good day's business at a fair, disposed of all his goods, and filled his purse with gold and silver. Afterwards he strapped his bag with the money in it onto his horse's back and rode off to try to make it home by the evening. **At noon** he stopped to rest in a small town, but when he was about to set out again, the stable-boy who brought his horse said: "Sir, you should **replace** the nail in the shoe on the left hind foot of your animal." "**Don't worry about it**," replied the tradesman. "**I am in a hurry** and the horseshoe will surely hold the six hours I have yet to travel."

Late in the afternoon he had to dismount again to feed his horse, and at this place also the boy came and told him that one of the shoes needed a new nail, and asked him whether he should take the horse to be fitted. "No, no, don't worry about it!" replied the master. "Surely **it will last** the couple of hours that I have now to travel. I am in a hurry." So he rode off; but his horse soon began **to limp**, and then it went from limping to stumbling, and finally the beast fell down and **broke its leg**. Thereupon the tradesman had to leave his unfortunate horse lying on the road, unbuckle his bag, and walk home with it upon his **shoulder**, where he arrived at last late at night.

"And all this misfortune," said he to himself, "is owing to one little nail. Being in a hurry was what really slowed me down!"

EL CLAVO

Un día un artesano tuvo una excelente jornada en la feria, vendió toda su mercancía y llenó su saca con oro y plata. Después ató la bolsa con el dinero al lomo de su caballo y emprendió el regreso a casa con la intención de llegar antes del anochecer. **A mediodía** se detuvo a descansar en una pequeña aldea y, cuando de nuevo iba a partir, el mozo de la cuadra que le trajo su caballo le dijo: «Señor, debe **reemplazar** el clavo de la pata trasera izquierda de su animal». «**No te preocupes** –respondió el artesano–. **Tengo prisa** y seguro que el zapato aguanta las seis horas de viaje que aún me quedan».

A última hora de la tarde volvió a descabalgar para alimentar al caballo, y también en este lugar el mozo le dijo que uno de los zapatos necesitaba un nuevo clavo, y le preguntó si debía llevar al caballo para que repararan el daño. «¡No, no te preocupes! –exclamó el hombre–. Seguro que **aguanta** el par de horas que me quedan. Tengo prisa». Y partió; pero al poco el caballo comenzó a **cojear,** después pasó de cojear a trastabillarse, para finalmente caer y **romperse la pata**. Por tanto, el artesano tuvo que dejar al desgraciado caballo tumbado en la carretera, desatar la saca y caminar con ella al **hombro** hasta casa, adonde por fin llegó bien entrada la noche.

«Y toda esta mala suerte a causa de un pequeño clavo. ¡Las prisas han sido las que realmente me han causado el retraso!».

THE THREE SPINNERS

There was once a **lazy** maiden who would not spin flax. Her **fed up** mother began to scream at the girl, and at that very instant, the queen drove by, stopped her carriage and asked the mother why there was so much screaming. The mother **felt ashamed of** her daughter's laziness, so **she lied**: "Oh, Your Majesty, she simply will not stop spinning!" The queen immediately offered to take the girl home with her so that she could spin all she liked. When they arrived at the castle, the queen showed the girl to three rooms filled with the finest flax. "Now spin me this flax," said the queen, "and you shall marry my oldest son." The maiden was filled with fear and began to cry so hard that three old women stopped below her window **to ask what was the matter.** The first woman had a great broad foot, the second had a large under-lip, and the third had an enormous thumb. The women offered to spin the flax for her if the maiden promised to invite them to the royal wedding. The maiden agreed and the three women quickly **got to work.** When they were done, the queen immediately made plans for the wedding. **As promised**, the bride invited the three women and introduced them to the groom as her aunts. "Alas!" exclaimed the groom, "how is it you have such ugly **relations**?" and going up to the one with a broad foot, he asked: "Why have you such a broad foot?" "From threading," she answered. Then he went to the second, and asked: "Why have you such an overhanging lip?" "From moistening the thread," she replied. Then he askcd the third: "Why have you such a big thumb?" "From pressing the thread," she answered. Then the prince became frightened, and said: "My lovely bride shall never touch another spinning wheel for as long as she lives!" Thus the maiden was freed from the hated task of spinning.

LAS TRES HILANDERAS

Había una vez una doncella **perezosa** que no quería hilar lino. **Harta**, su madre comenzó a gritar a la chica, y en aquel preciso instante pasó por allí la reina, que detuvo su coche y preguntó a la madre el porqué de aquel griterío. La madre **se sintió avergonzada** de la vaguería de su hija, y **mintió**: «Oh, Su Alteza, ¡mi hija no para de hilar!». Sin dudarlo, la reina se ofreció llevarse consigo a la chica para que hilase todo lo que quisiera. Cuando llegaron al castillo, la reina le mostró a la chica tres habitaciones repletas del mejor lino. «Si hilas este lino para mí, te casarás con el mayor de mis hijos», le dijo la reina. La doncella estaba aterrada, y empezó a llorar tan fuerte que tres ancianas se detuvieron bajo su ventana **para preguntarle cuál era el problema**. La primera mujer tenía un pie anchísimo; la segunda, un enorme labio inferior, y la tercera, un pulgar desmesurado. Las mujeres se ofrecieron a hilar el lino por ella, si las invitaba a la boda real. La doncella aceptó, y rápidamente las mujeres **comenzaron a trabajar**. Cuando terminaron, la reina comenzó los preparativos para la boda de inmediato. **Como había prometido**, la novia invitó a las tres mujeres y se las presentó a su prometido como sus tías. «¡Vaya! –exclamó el novio–, ¿cómo es que tienes unas **familiares** tan feas?», y dirigiéndose a la mujer con el pie ancho, le preguntó: «¿Por qué tiene el pie tan ancho?». «De enhebrar», respondió. Entonces se dirigió a la segunda y le preguntó: «¿Por qué tiene un labio que le cuelga?». «De humedecer el hilo», respondió. Por último, se dirigió a la tercera: «¿Por qué tiene un pulgar tan grande?». «De presionar el hilo», fue la respuesta. Entonces el príncipe se asustó y exclamó: «¡Mi querida princesa no volverá a tocar un rueca para el resto de sus días!». Y así fue como la doncella se libró de su odiada tarea.

TOADS AND DIAMONDS

A bad-tempered **widow** had two daughters. The eldest was like her mother, both in appearance and disposition, while the youngest resembled her father. She was sweet-natured always, and as pretty as she was amiable. The widow doted on the eldest, but had no love for the other, who she forced **to work hard** all day. Among her other hard tasks, she was forced to carry water from a distant fountain. One day **when she had just** filled her pitcher at the fountain, an old woman asked to drink from it. "Of course," replied the beautiful girl. "Your face is pretty and your heart is gentle," said she. "For your **kindness** to a poor old woman, I will give you a gift. Every time you speak, from your mouth shall come a flower or a jewel." When the girl reached home her mother **scolded her** for taking so long. "**Forgive me**," she sweetly replied. As she spoke some pearls and diamonds fell from her lips. "What is this I see, child?" asked the astonished widow. The forlorn girl eagerly related her experience with the old woman at the fountain, while, with her words, she dropped precious stones and roses. The widow immediately sent her favorite daughter to the fountain. Soon the old woman appeared and asked the girl for a drink from her pitcher, but the girl **refused**. "I will make you a gift," she said, "to equal your discourtesy and ill breeding. **Every time** you speak, there shall come from your mouth a snake or a toad." When the girl got home she opened her mouth and, to her mother's horror, two vipers and two toads sprang from it. The younger sister ran to the forest to escape her mother's wrath and wept bitterly. The king's son found her thus, and asked the cause of her tears. When se began to speak, pearls and diamonds fell from her lips. Enraptured, the prince asked her to marry him. Meanwhile the selfish sister and her mother lived together miserably until the end of their days.

SAPOS Y DIAMANTES

Una **viuda** de mal carácter tenía dos hijas. La mayor era como su madre, tanto en apariencia como de carácter, mientras que la más joven era como su padre: siempre afable, y tan guapa como sociable. La viuda se volcaba con la mayor, pero detestaba a la otra, a la que obligaba a **trabajar duramente** todo el día. Una de las arduas tareas era acarrear agua desde una lejana fuente. Un día, **cuando acababa de** llenar el cántaro en la fuente, una anciana le pidió beber de él. «Por supuesto», respondió la bella joven. «Tienes una cara bonita y un corazón benévolo –le dijo–. Por tu **bondad** hacia una anciana, te concedo un regalo. Cada vez que hables, brotará de tu boca una flor o una joya». Cuando la joven regresó a casa, su madre **le riñó** por haberse retrasado. «Perdóname», respondió con dulzura, y mientras hablaba salían perlas y diamantes de su boca. «¿Qué es esto, niña?», preguntó la viuda asombrada. La desamparada joven le contó entusiasmada lo ocurrido con la anciana en la fuente, mientras, al tiempo que palabras, dejaba caer piedras preciosas y rosas. De inmediato la viuda mandó a su hija favorita a por agua. Una vez allí se apareció la anciana y le pidió que le dejara beber de la jarra, pero la chica **se negó**. «Te premiaré con un regalo –le dijo– que iguale tu grosería y mala educación. **Cada vez** que hables saldrá de tu boca una serpiente o un sapo». Al llegar a casa la chica abrió la boca y, para espanto de su madre, de ella salieron dos víboras y dos sapos. La hermana menor corrió al bosque para escapar de la ira de su madre y se puso a llorar amargamente. Así la encontró el hijo del rey, que se interesó por la causa de su llanto. Al empezar a responder, de la boca de la joven salieron perlas y diamantes. Arrebatado, el príncipe le pidió que se casara con él. Mientras, la hermana egoísta y su madre vivieron juntas miserablemente hasta el final de sus días.

THE SWEET SOUP

Once upon a time there was a poor but very good little girl, who lived **alone** with her mother. They had nothing in the house to eat, and they were **both** very hungry. So the child went out into the forest, and there she met an old woman, who **already** knew her distress. She gave the little girl a **pot** which had the following power. If one said to it, "Boil, little pot!" it would cook sweet soup; and when one said: "Stop, little pot!" it would immediately cease to boil. The little girl took the pot home to her mother, and their **poverty** and **troubles** were at an end, for they could have soup as often as they pleased.

One day, however, the little girl went out, and in her absence the mother said: "Boil, little pot!" So it began to cook, and she **soon** ate all she wished; but when the poor woman wanted to have the pot stop, she found she did not know the words to make this happen. Therefore, the pot just kept boiling and boiling, and soon broth was falling over the edge. As it boiled and boiled the kitchen became full, then the house, and the next house, and soon the whole street. The entire village tried to stop the pot from boiling, but **no one knew how**. At last, when only a very small cottage at the edge of the village was left unfilled with soup, the child returned and said at once: "Stop, little pot!"

Immediately it ceased to boil; but whoever wishes to enter the village now must eat his way through the soup!!!

LA SOPA DULCE

Había una vez una niña pobre, pero muy buena, que vivía **sola** con su madre. En la casa no había nada para comer, y **ambas** estaban muy hambrientas. Así que la niña se adentró en el bosque, donde se encontró a una anciana que **ya** conocía su desgracia. La anciana le entregó a la niña una **olla** que tenía el siguiente poder: si alguien le decía: «¡Cuece, pequeña olla!», cocinaría una rica sopa. Y cuando alguien dijera: «Para, pequeña olla», inmediatamente dejaría de cocer. La joven llevó la olla a su madre, y su **pobreza** y **sus desdichas** terminaron, pues podrían comer sopa tan a menudo como quisieran.

Sin embargo, un día la niña salió de la casa y, en su ausencia, la madre dijo: «¡Cuece, pequeña olla!». La olla empezó a cocer, y **pronto** la madre pudo hartarse de comer; pero cuando la mujer quiso que la olla parara, no pudo encontrar las palabras para hacerlo. Así que la olla continuó cociendo y cociendo, y pronto la sopa comenzó a salirse de la olla. Al cocer y cocer, pronto la cocina se inundó, luego toda la casa, y la casa de al lado, y al poco toda la calle. Toda la aldea intentó que la olla parase, pero **nadie sabía cómo**. Por fin, cuando solamente una pequeña cabaña quedaba a salvo en un extremo de la aldea, la niña regresó y exclamó: «¡Para, pequeña olla!».

La olla se detuvo de inmediato; pero quien quiera visitar la aldea ahora ¡debe ir comiendo sopa para poder entrar!

WHY THE BEAR HAS A STUMPY TAIL

One winter's day the bear met the fox, who came slinking along with a string of fish **he had stolen**. "Hey, **wait! Where did you get those?**" demanded the bear.

"Oh, Mr. Bear, I've been out **fishing** and caught them," said the fox.

So the bear wanted to learn to fish, too, and asked the fox to tell him how he was to set about it.

"Oh, it is quite easy," answered the fox, "and soon learned. You've only got to go out on the ice, cut a hole and stick your **tail** down through it, and hold it there **as long as possible**. Don't worry if it hurts a little; that's what it feels like when the fish bite. The longer you hold it there, the more fish you'll get. Then you must pull your tail out quickly with all your might."

Well, the bear did as the fox said, and though he felt very cold, and his tail hurt very much, he kept it a long, long time down in the hole, until at last it was completely frozen, though **he did not know that**. Then he pulled it out with all his might, and it snapped right off, and that's why the bear wanders around with a stumpy tail **to this day**!

POR QUÉ EL OSO TIENE UNA COLA ACHAPARRADA

Un día de invierno el oso se encontró con el zorro, que venía con unos cuantos peces atados a una cuerda **que había robado**. «¡Hola, **espera! ¿De dónde los has sacado?**», le preguntó el oso.

«Ah, señor Oso, he ido a **pescar** y los he atrapado», respondió el zorro. Así que el oso quiso aprender a pescar también, y le pidió al zorro que le enseñara.

«Es muy fácil –contestó el zorro– y se aprende rápido. Solo tienes que subirte a una placa de hielo, hacer un agujero, meter la **cola** y dejarla allí **el mayor tiempo posible**. No te preocupes si te duele un poco, eso es lo que se siente cuando un pez pica. Cuanto más tiempo la dejes allí, más peces conseguirás. Por último debes sacar la cola rápidamente con todas tus fuerzas».

Así que el oso siguió los consejos del zorro, y aunque sentía mucho frío y la cola le dolía muchísimo, la dejó en el agujero durante largo rato, hasta que quedó completamente congelada, aunque **eso él no lo sabía**. Entonces dio un tirón con todas sus fuerzas para sacar la cola, y esta se partió, ¡y por eso **hasta el día de hoy** los osos vagan de un lado a otro con una cola achaparrada!

THE THREE LITTLE PIGS

Once upon a time, when pigs could talk and **no one had ever heard of** bacon, there lived an old piggy mother with her three little sons **in the middle of** a forest. One day she called her sons to her, and, **with tears in her eyes,** told them that she must send them out into the world to seek their fortune. One of the pigs found some straw and built a very nice house for himself. But soon a wolf came along and **knocked on the door** and said, "Little pig, little pig, let me in." But the little pig laughed and answered: "No, not by the hair on my chinny-chin-chin." Then said the wolf sternly: "Then I'll huff, and I'll puff, and I'll blow your house in!" And since the house was only made of straw, the wolf quickly blew down the walls and ate up the little pig. The second little pig soon built a nice little house made of sticks. It was **barely** finished when the same wolf came along, and presently blew this house in, too, and gobbled the pig right up. But the third little pig used **bricks** to build a strong house. As soon as it was finished the wolf came to call and said: "Little pig, little pig, let me in!" But the little pig answered: "No, not by the hair of my chinny-chin-chin." "Then," said the wolf, "I'll huff, and I'll puff, and I'll blow your house in."

But no matter how hard he huffed and puffed, he could not blow this house down. At last he decided to climb down the **chimney,** but the clever pig had already hung a pot full of boiling water over the hearth. Just as the wolf was coming down the chimney he took off the cover and in fell the wolf. The little pig then popped the lid on again **as soon as he could**.

Then he boiled the wolf, and ate him for supper, and after that he lived quietly and comfortably all his days, and was never troubled by a wolf again.

LOS TRES CERDITOS

Había una vez, cuando los cerdos podían hablar y **nadie había oído hablar del** beicon, una cerda anciana que vivía con sus tres hijos **en medio del** bosque. Un día llamó a sus hijos a su presencia y les dijo **con lágrimas en los ojos** que debía mandarles por el mundo en busca de fortuna. Uno de los cerditos encontró algo de paja y se construyó una estupenda casa. Pero pronto un lobo llegó hasta allí, **llamó a la puerta** y dijo: «Cerdito, cerdito, déjame entrar». El cerdito se rio y respondió: «No, no, ni pensarlo». Entonces el lobo respondió secamente: «Pues soplaré y soplaré y derribaré tu casa». Y como la casa estaba solamente hecha de paja, el lobo la derribó con mucha facilidad y se comió al cerdito. El segundo cerdito pronto consiguió construir una nueva casa hecha de palillos. **Apenas** había terminado cuando llegó el mismo lobo y, rápidamente, derribó esa casa también y se tragó al cerdito en un instante. El tercer cerdito construyó su casa con **ladrillos** para hacerla robusta. Apenas terminó se acercó el lobo y le dijo: «¡Cerdito, cerdito, déjame entrar!». Pero el cerdito se negó: «¡Ni pensarlo!». «Entonces soplaré y soplaré y derribaré tu casa», respondió el lobo.

Pero por mucho que soplara, no conseguía derribar la casa. Por fin decidió descender por la **chimenea,** pero el cerdito, muy listo, había puesto una olla llena de agua hirviendo al fuego. Mientras el lobo descendía la chimenea, el cerdito retiró la tapa de la olla y allí cayó el lobo. **Tan pronto como pudo**, el cerdito volvió a colocar la tapa.

El cerdito coció al lobo y se lo comió para cenar, y ya tranquilo vivió feliz el resto de sus días, sin que ningún lobo lo molestara de nuevo.

PUSS IN BOOTS

There was once a miller, who was so poor that at his death he had nothing to leave to his son, Jack, but his cat, Puss. "Though Puss may feed himself by catching mice," Jack sighed, "I shall die of hunger." The cat overheard his young master, and began to speak. "Dear master," said he, "If you buy me a pair of boots and give me an old bag, **you'll see what I am capable of.**" Now, Jack was very poor, but he **trusted** Puss and spent all he had on a nice pair of boots. Puss immediately used the bag to catch **rabbits**, partridges and other animals for them to eat. Every day Puss would take partridges or hares to the royal palace, always with the same message: "From my Lord the Marquis of Carabas." Finally Puss decided that **it was time** for his master to be introduced at court, so he **persuaded** him to go and bathe in a nearby river, having heard that the king would soon pass that way. Jack stood shivering up to his neck in water, wondering what was to happen next, when suddenly the king's carriage appeared in sight. At once Puss began to call out as loudly as he could: "Help, help! My Lord the Marquis of Carabas **is drowning!**" The king recognized the cat and ordered his attendants to go to the assistance of the Marquis. Puss ran to the king and told him that some **thieves** had run off with his master's clothes while he was bathing. The king instantly sent one of his men to fetch a handsome suit of purple and gold from the royal wardrobe. Jack, who was a fine, handsome fellow, looked so well in the suit that everyone believed he was a noble foreign lord.

The king and his daughter were so pleased with his appearance that they invited him into their carriage, where Jack and the princess immediately **fell in love**. And so the miller's son married the king's daughter, and there were great rejoicings throughout the land.

EL GATO CON BOTAS

Había una vez un molinero que era tan pobre que al morir no tenía nada más que su gato, Puss, para dejarle a su hijo, Juan, en herencia. «Tal vez Puss pueda alimentarse si caza un ratón –suspiró Juan–, pero yo moriré de hambre». El gato oyó a su joven dueño y comenzó a hablar: «Querido jefe, si me compras un par de botas y me das una bolsa vieja, **verás de lo que soy capaz**». Juan era muy pobre, pero **confió en** Puss y se gastó todo lo que tenía en un buen par de botas. De inmediato Puss usó la bolsa para cazar **conejos**, perdices y otros animales para comérselos. Cada día Puss llevaba perdices o liebres al palacio real, siempre con el mismo mensaje: «De parte de mi señor, el Marqués de Carabás». Pasado un tiempo Puss decidió que **había llegado el momento** en que su señor fuese presentado en la corte, así que **convenció** a Juan de que fuera a bañarse a un río cercano, pues había oído que pronto el rey pasaría por allí. Juan se mantuvo tiritando en el río con el agua hasta el cuello, y se preguntaba qué pasaría después, cuando de pronto apareció a la vista el coche del rey. De inmediato, Puss comenzó a gritar tan alto como pudo: «¡Ayuda, ayuda! Mi señor el Marqués de Carabás **se ahoga!**». El rey reconoció al gato y ordenó a sus asistentes que ayudaran al Marqués. Puss corrió hacia el rey y le contó que unos **ladrones** habían escapado corriendo con las ropas de su señor mientras se bañaba. Sin perder un minuto, el rey mandó a uno de los suyos a buscar un bonito traje púrpura y oro del armario real. Juan, que era un joven bien parecido, estaba tan elegante con el traje que todos pensaron que era un noble extranjero.

El rey y su hija estaban tan satisfechos con su aspecto que lo invitaron a subirse al coche con ellos, donde Juan y la princesa **se enamoraron** al instante. Y así fue como el hijo del molinero se casó con la hija del rey, y hubo grandes celebraciones por todo el reino.

THE ELVES AND THE SHOEMAKER

There was once a shoemaker who, **through no fault of his own**, had become so poor that at last he had only enough leather left for one pair of shoes. At evening he cut out the shoes which he intended to start making the next morning, lay down quietly, **said his prayers**, and fell asleep. In the morning when he was preparing to sit down to work, he found the pair of shoes standing finished on his table. He was amazed, and could not understand it **at all**. He took the shoes in his hand to examine them more closely. They were so neatly sewn that not a stitch was out of place and were as good as the work of a master-hand. Soon a purchaser came in and paid more than the ordinary price for them, so that the shoemaker was able to buy leather for two pairs with the money. He cut them out in the evening, and the next day when he woke up, the shoes were finished, and buyers were not lacking. These gave him so much money that he was able to buy leather for four pairs of shoes. Early the next morning he found the four pairs finished, and so it went. **Eventually** he became a well-to-do man. One evening he said to his wife: "Should we sit up tonight to see who it is that **lends us such a helping hand?**" The wife agreed, and they hid themselves **in the corner** of the room behind some hanging clothes. **At midnight** they saw how two little naked men worked hard to finish making all the shoes. **In gratitude**, the shoemaker and his wife decided to make little clothes and shoes for the elves. When they found their new clothes laid out for them the following night, the elves felt so fine that they skipped away and never made shoes again. But the shoemaker fared well as long as he lived, and had good luck in everything he did.

LOS ELFOS Y EL ZAPATERO

Había una vez un zapatero que, **sin tener ninguna culpa**, llegó un momento en el que solo le quedaba cuero para un par de zapatos. Llegada la noche, cortó los zapatos que pretendía comenzar a hacer a la mañana siguiente, se tumbó en silencio, **rezó** y se durmió. Por la mañana, al ir a sentarse para empezar a trabajar, descubrió los zapatos terminados encima de la mesa. El zapatero estaba maravillado y no entendía aquello **en absoluto**. Sostuvo los zapatos en su mano para examinarlos con más detalle. Estaban cosidos tan primorosamente que no había ni una puntada fuera de sitio, y eran de tanta calidad como los fabricados por la mano del artesano más experto. Poco después llegó un cliente y pagó un precio más alto del habitual por ellos, así que con ese dinero el zapatero pudo comprar cuero para dos pares de zapatos. Al llegar la noche, cortó los zapatos y, al día siguiente, cuando se despertó, estaban terminados y no les faltaban compradores. Esto le permitió ganar tanto dinero como para comprar cuero para cuatro pares de zapatos. A primera hora de la mañana siguiente encontró los cuatro pares terminados, y así continuó. **Con el tiempo** se convirtió en un hombre adinerado. Una noche le preguntó a su esposa: «¿Deberíamos quedarnos despiertos esta noche para ver quién **nos echa una mano?**». La mujer estuvo de acuerdo, y ambos se escondieron **en un rincón** de la habitación, bajo algunas ropas. **A medianoche** vieron cómo dos pequeños hombres desnudos trabajaron duramente para acabar los zapatos. **Como agradecimiento**, el zapatero y su esposa decidieron fabricar zapatos y ropas para los elfos. Cuando la noche siguiente los elfos encontraron sus nuevas ropas, se sintieron tan bien con ellas que escaparon y nunca más volvieron a fabricar zapatos. Sin embargo, al zapatero le fue bien el resto de su vida y tuvo suerte en todo lo que hizo.

BELLING THE CAT

Once upon a time the mice talked of how they might outwit their enemy, the cat. But **good advice was scarce**, and in vain the president called upon all the most experienced mice to find a way. At last a very young mouse held up two fingers and asked to be allowed to speak, and said: "**I've been thinking for a long time** about why the cat is such a **dangerous** enemy. Now, it's not so much because of her quickness, though people make so much fuss about that. If we could only notice her in time, I've no doubt we're nimble enough to jump into our holes before she could do us any harm. It's in her **velvet** paws; that's where she hides her cruel claws till she gets us in her clutches—that's where her power lies. With those paws she can tread so lightly that we can't hear her coming. And so, while we are still dancing heedlessly about the place, she creeps close up, and before we know where we are she pounces down on us and has us in her clutches. I believe we ought to hang a **bell** around her neck to warn us of her coming while there's still time." Everyone applauded this proposal, and the council decided that it should be carried out. Now the question to be settled was, who should undertake to fasten the bell round the cat's neck? The president declared that no one could be better fitted for the task than he who had come up with such an excellent idea. But at that the young mouse became quite confused and **stammered** an excuse. He was too young for the deed, he said. He didn't know the cat well enough. His grandfather, who knew her better, would be more suited to the job. But the grandfather declared that because he knew the cat very well he would take good care not to attempt such a task. And **the long and the short of it** was that no other mouse would undertake the duty; and so this clever proposal was never carried out, and the cat remained mistress of the situation.

PONERLE EL CASCABEL AL GATO

Había una vez unos ratones que hablaban de cómo doblegar a su **enemigo**, el gato. Sin embargo, **las buenas ideas escaseaban**, y en vano el presidente mandó llamar a los ratones más experimentados para encontrar una solución. Por fin un ratón muy joven levantó dos dedos y pidió permiso para hablar, y dijo: «**Llevo mucho tiempo pensando** por qué el gato es tan **peligroso**. Bien, no es tanto por su rapidez, aunque la gente lo crea así. Si pudiéramos percibirlo a tiempo, no dudo de que seríamos lo suficientemente ágiles como para llegar hasta nuestros agujeros antes de que pudiera hacernos daño. En sus patas de **terciopelo**, ahí es donde esconde sus crueles garras hasta que estamos a su alcance, esa es su fuerza. Con esas patas puede pisar tan sigilosamente que no podemos oírlo. Y por eso mientras bailamos como locos, se acerca sin hacer ruido, y antes de que nos demos cuenta se lanza sobre nosotros y nos atrapa entre sus garras. Creo que debemos colgarle un **cascabel** en el cuello para que nos avise a tiempo de que se acerca». Todos aplaudieron esta idea, y el consejo decidió que se llevara a cabo. El problema era decidir quién debía atar el cascabel en el cuello del gato. El presidente afirmó que no había nadie más apto que aquel al que se le había ocurrido una idea tan buena. Sin embargo, el joven ratón quedó desconcertado por la propuesta y **balbuceó** una excusa. Era demasiado joven para el encargo, dijo. No conocía al gato lo suficientemente bien. Su abuelo, que lo conocía mejor, sería mucho más adecuado. Pero el abuelo alegó que dado que conocía al gato tan bien, tendría buen cuidado de no llevar a cabo la tarea. Y **el caso es que** ningún otro ratón quiso encargarse del cometido, por lo que la inteligente propuesta nunca se llevó a cabo, y el gato siguió siendo el amo de la situación.

JACK AND THE BEANSTALK

Once upon a time there lived a poor widow who had an **only son** named Jack. One day she asked Jack to go to market to sell their only possession, a sick old cow which no longer gave milk. When Jack had only walked a short way, he ran into a butcher, who he told of his plan to sell the cow at market. "It's lucky I met you," the butcher said. "You may save yourself the trouble of going so far." He put his hand in his **pocket**, and pulled out five curious-looking beans. "These are the most wonderful beans that ever were known. If you plant them at night, by the next morning they'll grow up and reach the sky. I will give them to you for that cow of yours." Jack accepted and ran all the way home to tell his mother. How **disappointed** the poor widow was! "**Off to bed with you!**" she cried and threw the magic beans out the window into the garden. The next morning, Jack found a huge beanstalk, which stretched up into the sky. He jumped onto the stalk and climbed until he found himself in a new and beautiful country. There he saw a giant's **castle,** with a broad road leading straight up to the front gate. As he drew near to the castle, he saw the giant's wife standing at the door. "Would you kindly give me some breakfast?" he asked. The giant's wife had a kind heart, so she made him a hearty breakfast. But when her cruel husband came home, she quickly **hid** Jack. "I smell the blood of a young man!" screamed the giant and looked around for the little boy, but he couldn't find him. So he sat down for breakfast and asked his wife to bring him two bags full of gold. The giant soon became so sleepy that **his head began to nod** and he began **to snore**. Then Jack crept out, snatched up the two bags and climbed down the beanstalk back to his mother's cottage before the giant awoke. And so it was that Jack and his mother grew very rich, and lived happy ever after.

JUAN Y LAS HABICHUELAS

Había una vez una pobre viuda que tenía un **único hijo** llamado Juan. Un día le pidió a Juan que fuera al mercado a vender su único bien, una vaca enferma y vieja que ya no daba leche. Apenas acababa de salir Juan cuando se encontró con un carnicero al que le contó su plan de vender la vaca en el mercado. «Qué suerte haberte encontrado —le dijo el carnicero—. Puede que te ahorres tener que ir hasta allí», y sacó de su **bolsillo** cinco habichuelas de aspecto extraño. «Estas son las habichuelas más extraordinarias jamás conocidas. Si las plantas de noche, al día siguiente crecerán hasta tocar el cielo. Te las cambio por tu vaca». Juan aceptó, y corrió de vuelta a casa para contárselo a su madre. ¡Qué **desilusión** se llevó la pobre viuda! «**Vete ahora mismo a la cama**», gritó, y tiró las habichuelas al jardín por la ventana. A la mañana siguiente, Juan encontró una enorme planta que crecía hasta el cielo. Se subió a la planta y comenzó a escalar hasta que se encontró en un nuevo y hermoso país. Allí vio el **castillo** de un gigante, hasta cuya puerta conducía una ancha carretera. Cuando estuvo más cerca del castillo, vio a la mujer del gigante a la puerta. «¿Serías tan amable de darme algo de desayunar?», le preguntó. La mujer del gigante tenía un buen corazón, así que le preparó un abundante desayuno. Pero cuando su cruel marido regresó a casa, la mujer **escondió** rápidamente a Juan. «¡Huelo la sangre de un jovencito!», gritó el gigante, y buscó al niño por los alrededores sin encontrarlo. Así que el gigante se sentó a desayunar y le pidió a su mujer que le trajera dos bolsas repletas de oro. Pronto al gigante le entró tanto sueño que empezó **a dar cabezadas** y **roncar**. Entonces Juan salió, agarró las bolsas y bajó por la planta hasta la casa de su madre antes de que el gigante se despertase. Y así fue como Juan y su madre se volvieron muy ricos y vivieron muy felices para siempre.

SLEEPING BEAUTY

Long ago a king and queen had a baby daughter, and they held a great festival throughout the kingdom to celebrate **the birth** of the princess. Among the **guests** were seven very powerful **fairies**, whom the queen was very anxious to please. They were just sitting down to dinner when, **all of a sudden**, a black cloud appeared in the room. In came an old fairy dressed in black and stalked up to the table. The king and queen had forgotten to invite the spiteful fairy Tormentilla, who placed a curse on the **newborn** princess. "And I say that she shall prick her hand with a spindle and die of the wound!" The queen wept bitterly until one little fairy came forward and said: "**Do not cry,** dear queen; I cannot quite undo this wicked spell, but I can promise you that your daughter shall not die, but only fall asleep for a hundred years. Then a prince shall come and awaken her with a kiss." So the king and queen **dried their tears** and things went on much as usual in the palace. But when the princess was almost eighteen years old, she pricked her finger on a spindle, and she and the entire kingdom fell into a deep sleep. After a hundred years had passed, the palace and the story of it were all but forgotten until one day a prince came upon the palace. There everyone was sleeping, but the most spectacular site was the lovely sleeping lady. She was so beautiful that to see her almost **took his breath away** and, falling on his knees, he bent to kiss her. As he kissed her, she opened her lovely blue eyes and said, smiling: "Oh! prince, have you come at last? I have had such pleasant dreams." And, all at the same time, the whole palace was awake. The prince and the princess were married, and the entire kingdom rejoiced.

LA BELLA DURMIENTE

Hace mucho tiempo un rey y una reina tuvieron una hija, y organizaron una gran fiesta en todo el reino para celebrar **el nacimiento** de la princesa. Entre los **invitados** había siete poderosas **hadas**, a las que la reina estaba deseosa de agradar. Acababan de sentarse a cenar cuando, **de pronto**, apareció una nube negra en el comedor. En ella llegó una anciana hada vestida de negro que se acercó a la mesa. El rey y la reina habían olvidado invitar a la malévola hada Tormentilla, que lanzó una maldición sobre la princesa **recién nacida**: «Y digo que se punzará la mano con una rueca y morirá a causa de la herida». La reina se puso a llorar desconsoladamente hasta que una pequeña hada se acercó y dijo: «**No llore**, querida reina, no puedo deshacer el malvado hechizo, pero le prometo que su hija no morirá, solo caerá dormida durante cien años. Entonces vendrá un príncipe y la despertará con un beso». El rey y la reina **se secaron las lágrimas** y la normalidad volvió al palacio. Sin embargo, cuando la princesa estaba a punto de cumplir dieciocho años, se punzó el dedo con una rueca y ella y el reino entero cayeron en un profundo sueño. Pasados cien años, el palacio y su leyenda habían caído en el olvido, hasta que un día un príncipe se acercó al palacio. Allí todos dormían, pero lo más espectacular era la joven belleza durmiente. Era tan preciosa que casi **le deja sin aliento** y, cayendo de rodillas, la besó. En el momento en que la besó, la princesa abrió sus bellos ojos azules y dijo sonriendo: «¡Oh, príncipe!, ¿por fin has llegado? He tenido unos sueños tan hermosos». Y al mismo tiempo todo el palacio despertó. El príncipe y la princesa se casaron, y el reino entero lo celebró.

BEAUTY AND THE BEAST

There was once a merchant who had a young daughter who was known for her beauty. She was so beautiful that people began to call her Beauty. In addition to her loveliness, Beauty was also **hardworking**, intelligent and **loved to read**. Many men wanted to marry Beauty, but she always told them that she was too young to marry and preferred to stay with her father a little longer. One stormy evening Beauty's father **got lost** in a neighboring country and took refuge in an enchanted palace. When morning came he **plucked a rose** to give to his daughter Beauty, but just then a beast appeared and angrily screamed: "Why are you stealing my roses after I was so kind to you last night? Now you must stay here as my **prisoner**." When the merchant explained that the rose was for his daughter, the beast agreed to let him leave under the condition that Beauty would come to live with him at the enchanted palace. **At first** Beauty was afraid of the beast, but she soon saw that he was a kind man. Every night the beast asked Beauty to marry him, but Beauty always said no. He was so in love with her that he finally allowed her to go visit her sick father. Beauty promised to return within a week, but she was detained for a few extra days with her father. When she returned to the palace, she found the beast lying on the floor of the garden. Beauty was so sad and full of grief that she fell to the ground and kissed the beast through a sea of tears. Suddenly Beauty noticed that the palace began **to sparkle**. When she looked down again she saw that her kiss of true love had turned the beast into one of the loveliest princes in the world. Beauty **looked everywhere for** the beast until the prince explained to her that her kiss had lifted a spell cast by a witch long ago. Beauty and the beast were married and lived happily ever after.

LA BELLA Y LA BESTIA

Había una vez un comerciante que tenía una hija famosa por su belleza. La niña era tan preciosa que desde pequeña la gente empezó a llamarla Bella. Además de su hermosura, Bella era muy **trabajadora** e inteligente, y **le encantaba leer**. Muchos jóvenes querían casarse con ella, pero Bella siempre respondía que era demasiado joven y que prefería quedarse con su padre un tiempo más. Un día el padre de Bella **se perdió** por los campos vecinos en medio de una tormenta y se refugió en un palacio encantado. Al amanecer **cortó una rosa** para su hija, pero en ese momento apareció una bestia que le gritó enfurecido: «¿Por qué robas mis rosas si anoche fui muy bueno contigo? A partir de ahora permanecerás aquí como mi **prisionero**». Cuando el comerciante le explicó que la rosa era para su hija, la bestia lo dejó marchar, a condición de que Bella viviese con él en el palacio encantado. **Al principio** Bella tenía miedo de la bestia, pero pronto se dio cuenta de que era un buen hombre. Cada noche la bestia le pedía a Bella que se casase con él, pero ella siempre se negaba. Él estaba tan enamorado de Bella que finalmente le permitió ir a visitar a su padre enfermo. Bella prometió regresar en una semana, pero tuvo que quedarse unos días más con su padre. Cuando volvió al palacio, encontró a la bestia tendida en el suelo del jardín. Bella se puso tan triste y llena de dolor que se dejó caer y besó a la bestia en un mar de lágrimas. De pronto Bella notó que el palacio comenzaba a **relucir**. Cuando volvió a mirar hacia abajo, vio que el beso de amor verdadero había transformado a la bestia en uno de los más bellos príncipes del mundo. Bella **buscó a la bestia por todas partes**, hasta que el príncipe le explicó que el beso había acabado con el maleficio que le había impuesto una bruja hacía mucho tiempo. Bella y la bestia se casaron y vivieron muy felices.

THE LITTLE RED HEN

Once upon a time there was a little red hen who lived with a pig, a duck and a cat. **They shared** a little house which the red hen liked to keep neat and clean. The little red hen worked hard all day long, but the others never helped. Although they said they would lend her a hand, they were far too lazy. One day the little red hen was working in the garden when she found a grain of corn. "**Who will help me** plant this corn?" she asked. "Not I," said the pig from his **mud puddle**. "Not I," quacked the duck from his pond. "Not I," said the cat from her spot in the sun. So the little red hen planted the grain of corn. First the corn grew into a tall green stalk, and then it ripened in the sun. When the time had come for cutting the corn, the little red hen asked her friends for help, but again they all said no. Her friends also refused to help her take the corn to the mill to be ground into **flour**, so the little red hen had to do this by herself, too. When the miller sent her a bag of flour, the little red hen asked her friends to help her make bread, but once again no one wanted to help her. So the little red hen mixed the flour into **dough**. She put it into the oven to bake, and soon there was a lovely smell of fresh bread. It filled the house and wafted out into the garden. When the little red hen opened the oven door, out came the most delicious looking loaf of bread she and her friends had ever seen. "Who is going to eat this bread?" she asked and all of her friends shouted, "I will! I will!" But the little red hen said, "I planted the seed, cut the corn, took it to the mill and made the bread, all by myself. Now I shall eat the loaf **all by myself.**" So the pig, the duck and the cat all stood and watched as the little red hen ate the entire loaf, right down to the very last **crumb.**

LA GALLINITA ROJA

Había una vez una gallinita roja que vivía con un cerdo, un pato y un gato. **Compartían** una casita que a la gallinita roja le gustaba tener limpia y reluciente. La gallinita roja trabajaba muy duro todo el día, pero los otros animales nunca ayudaban. Aunque los otros siempre decían que iban a echarle una mano, eran demasiado vagos. Estaba un día la gallinita roja trabajando en el jardín, cuando encontró un grano de maíz. «**¿Quién me ayudará** a plantar este grano?», preguntó la gallinita. «Yo no», contestó el cerdo desde el **charco de barro**. «Yo no», respondió el pato desde el estanque. «Yo no», dijo el gato tumbado al sol. Así que la gallinita roja plantó el grano de maíz. Primero el grano de maíz se convirtió en un enorme tallo verde, y luego maduró al sol. Cuando llegó el tiempo de segar el maíz, la gallinita roja pidió ayuda a sus amigos, pero de nuevo todos se negaron. Sus amigos también se negaron a ayudarle a llevar el maíz al molino para convertirlo en **harina**, así que de nuevo la gallinita roja tuvo que hacerlo ella misma. Cuando el molinero le mandó un saco de harina, la gallinita roja les pidió a sus amigos que le ayudaran a hacer el pan, pero una vez más nadie quiso ayudarla. Así que la gallinita roja convirtió la harina en **masa**. La metió en el horno para cocerla y muy pronto el aire se llenó de un riquísimo olor a pan tierno. El olor se propagó por la casa y salió al jardín. Cuando la gallinita roja abrió la puerta del horno, sacó de él el pan con la pinta más deliciosa que sus amigos y ella jamás hubieran visto. «¿Quién va a comerse este pan?», preguntó, y todos sus amigos exclamaron: «¡Yo! ¡Yo!». Pero la gallinita roja dijo: «Yo planté la semilla, segué el maíz, lo llevé al molino e hice el pan sin ayuda. Ahora me comeré el pan también **yo sola**». Y así el cerdo, el pato y el gato se quedaron para ver cómo la gallinita roja se comía todo el pan, hasta las últimas **migas**.

THE GREAT BIG TURNIP

Once upon a time an old man planted some turnip **seeds**. Each year he grew good turnips, but this year he was especially proud of one very big turnip. He **left it** in the ground longer than the others and watched with delight as it grew bigger and bigger. It grew so big that no one could remember ever having seen such a huge turnip before. At last it stopped growing, and the old man decided it was time **to pull it up**. He grabbed hold of the leaves and pulled with all his might, but the turnip would not move. So the man asked his wife to help him, and they both pulled and pulled **but it was no use**. So they asked their **granddaughter** for help and the three of them pulled and pulled, but the turnip still would not budge. The dog called the cat to come and help pull up the turnip. The cat pulled the dog, the dog pulled the granddaughter, the granddaughter pulled the old woman, the old woman pulled the old man, and the old man pulled the turnip. They all pulled as hard as they could, but still the turnip would not move. Then the cat called to the mouse to come help pull up the turnip. The mouse pulled the cat, the cat pulled the dog, the dog pulled the granddaughter, the granddaughter pulled the old woman, the old woman pulled the old man, and he pulled the turnip. **Together** they pulled and pulled **as hard as they could**. Suddenly, the enormous turnip came out of the ground, and **they all fell to the ground**!

EL NABO GIGANTE

Había una vez un viejo que plantó unas **semillas** de nabo. Cada año crecían buenos nabos, pero este año estaba especialmente orgulloso de un nabo extraordinariamente grande. El viejo **lo dejó** en la tierra más tiempo que al resto de los nabos, y miraba encantado cómo crecía y crecía. El nabo creció tanto que nadie recordaba haber visto un nabo tan grande jamás. Por fin dejó de crecer y el viejo decidió que había llegado el momento de **arrancarlo** de la tierra. El viejo agarró las hojas y tiró con todas su fuerzas, pero el nabo no se movió. El hombre pidió ayuda a su esposa, y juntos tiraron y tiraron, **pero sin ningún resultado**. Entonces pidieron ayuda a su **nieta**, pero a pesar de que tiraron los tres a la vez, el nabo no cedió. El perro le pidió al gato que viniera a ayudarles a tirar del nabo. El gato tiró del perro, el perro de la nieta, la nieta de la mujer, la mujer del viejo y el viejo del nabo. Todos tiraron tanto como pudieron, pero el nabo no se movió. Entonces el gato llamó al ratón para que les ayudara a arrancar el nabo. El ratón tiró del gato, el gato tiró del perro, el perro de la nieta, la nieta de la mujer, la mujer del viejo y el viejo del nabo. Todos **juntos** tiraron y tiraron **tan fuerte como pudieron**. De pronto el enorme nabo salió de la tierra ¡y **todos cayeron al suelo**!

BLUE BEARD

Once upon a time there was a very rich man who, **unfortunately,** had a blue beard. It made him look so ugly and terrible, there was not a woman or girl who did not run away from him. One of his neighbors had two beautiful daughters, and he proposed to marry one of them. Neither of the daughters, however, wanted to marry him. They also disliked him because they knew he had already been married several times, and **nobody knew what had become of** his wives. Blue Beard, in order to improve the acquaintance, took the girls with their mother to one of his country homes for **a week.** Immediately upon their return to town, he and the youngest daughter were married. A few months later, Bluebeard told his wife that he would be away for the next six weeks, and that she should amuse herself during his absence. "Here," said he to her, "are the keys to all of the rooms in the house. This little key opens the closet **at the end of** the hall on the ground floor. Open everything, and go everywhere except into that little closet, which **I forbid you to enter.**" Once her husband had gone away, the young bride could not control her curiosity about the forbidden room. With trembling fingers, she opened the lock and **was speechless** at what she found inside. There were all of Bluebeard's former wives locked up in a small prison! The terrified young bride quickly sent word for her brothers to come and free the women and defend her from her dreadful husband upon his return. But Bluebeard returned from his journey unexpectedly and **found out** that his wife knew his secret. **Just as he was about to** throw her into the prison with the rest of his poor wives, the young bride's brothers arrived. First they freed the other prisoners and then they threw Bluebeard into the prison. All of the wives took possession of Bluebeard's riches and went on to live long, happy lives.

BARBAZUL

Había una vez un hombre muy rico que, **por desgracia,** tenía una barba azul que le daba un aspecto feo y desagradable, y no había niña o mujer que no se alejara de él a toda prisa. Uno de sus vecinos tenía dos hijas preciosas y el hombre propuso casarse con una de ellas. Sin embargo, ninguna de las dos hijas quería casarse con él. Además les desagradaba que ya hubiese estado casado varias veces, aunque **nadie sabía qué había sido de** sus anteriores esposas. Barbazul, intentando ganarse el favor de las muchachas, invitó a las hermanas y a la madre a pasar una **semana** en una de sus casas de campo. En cuanto regresaron a la ciudad la hija menor se casó con él. Unos meses después, Barbazul le dijo a su mujer que se ausentaría durante las siguientes seis semanas, y que se divirtiera durante su ausencia: «Aquí están las llaves de todas las habitaciones de la casa —le dijo—. Esta llave pequeña abre la habitación **del final del** pasillo de la planta baja. Puedes abrir todas las puertas e ir donde te plazca, excepto a este pequeño cuarto, donde **te prohibo que entres**». Una vez que su marido se hubo marchado, la curiosidad acerca de la habitación prohibida venció a la muchacha. Con dedos temblorosos abrió el cerrojó, y **se quedó sin habla** ante lo que vio. Allí estaban todas las mujeres anteriores de Barbazul, ¡encerradas en una pequeña prisión! Aterrorizada, la joven envió a toda prisa un mensaje a sus hermanos para que vinieran a liberar a las mujeres y a defenderla a ella cuando llegara su terrible marido. Pero Barbazul regresó inesperadamente de su viaje y **supo** que ella conocía su secreto. **Cuando estaba a punto de** encerrarla con las otras desdichadas mujeres, llegaron los hermanos de la muchacha. Primero liberaron a las prisioneras y, después, encerraron a Barbazul en la habitación. Todas las mujeres se repartieron los bienes de Barbazul y vivieron felices durante muchos años.

THE FROG PRINCE

Once upon a time there lived a king whose daughter was so beautiful that the sun itself was astonished whenever it shone on her face. The young princess had a little golden ball, which she loved **to play** with by a well. One day her ball fell into the water. The princess began to cry, when she suddenly heard a strange **voice** say, "**What is wrong** little princess?" **She looked all around** to see who the voice was coming from, and saw a frog stretching forth its big, ugly head from the water. "Ah, it is you," she said, "I am weeping for my golden ball, which has fallen into the well." "I can bring it to you," answered the frog, "but **in exchange** I want you to let me be your companion." The princess promised to grant the frog's request, and shortly thereafter the frog brought her the ball. As soon as the princess picked up her ball, **she ran away**. The next day while the royal family was having dinner, the frog appeared. The princess quickly ran away from the frog, but when her father found out about the promise she had made he told her that true princesses always **keep their promises.** When the frog asked to be taken to her comfortable bed for a nap, she began to cry. But the king grew angry and said, "This frog helped you when you were in trouble, so you should not despise him now." So she took hold of the frog with two fingers, carried him upstairs, and put him in a corner. The frog **threatened** to tell her father how she was behaving. The princess was so angry that she picked up the frog and threw him against the wall with all of her might. But when he fell down, he was no frog but rather a prince with kind and beautiful eyes. Then he told her how he had been bewitched by a wicked witch, and how no one could have delivered him from the well but herself. In spite of herself, the princess fell madly in love with the prince and the two of them lived happily ever after.

EL PRÍNCIPE RANA

Había una vez un rey cuya hija era tan hermosa que hasta el propio sol se maravillaba cada vez que relucía en su cara. La joven princesa tenía una pequeña pelota de oro con la que le gustaba **jugar** junto a un pozo. Un día su pelota cayó al agua. La princesa empezó a llorar cuando, de pronto, oyó una **voz** que le decía: «**¿Qué sucede**, princesita?». **La joven miró alrededor** para ver de dónde procedía la voz, y vio que una rana sacaba del agua su fea y enorme cabeza. «Ah, eres tú –dijo ella–, lloro por mi pelota de oro, que ha caído al pozo». «Yo puedo traértela –contestó la rana–, pero **a cambio** quiero que me dejes hacerte compañía». La princesa le prometió a la rana atender su petición, y poco después la rana recuperó la pelota. Tan pronto como la princesa recuperó su pelota, **se marchó corriendo.** Al día siguiente, mientras la familia real cenaba, apareció la rana. Rápidamente la princesa salió huyendo de la rana, pero cuando su padre se enteró de la promesa que ella había hecho, le dijo que las verdaderas princesas siempre **mantenían sus promesas.** Cuando la rana le pidió que le llevara a su cómoda cama para echarse una siesta, la princesa comenzó a llorar. Sin embargo, el rey se enfadó y le dijo: «Esta rana te ayudó cuando estabas en apuros, así que ahora no debes despreciarla». De modo que la princesa agarró a la rana con dos dedos, la llevó escaleras arriba y la dejó en un rincón. La rana la **amenazó** con decirle a su padre cómo se estaba comportando. La princesa estaba tan furiosa que cogió a la rana y la lanzó contra la pared con todas sus fuerzas. Pero cuando cayó al suelo, ya no era una rana, sino un príncipe con unos ojos preciosos y llenos de bondad. Entonces él le contó cómo había sido hechizado por una bruja, y cómo nadie había podido sacarlo del pozo excepto ella. A pesar de su reticencia, la princesa se enamoró perdidamente del príncipe, y los dos vivieron felices para siempre.

THE GINGERBREAD MAN

One day an old woman was making some ginger-bread. She had some dough left over so she made **the shape** of a little man. She used red candies to make his eyes, nose and mouth and placed chocolates down his front to look like buttons. Then she placed him on a baking sheet and put him in the **oven** to bake. After a little while, she heard something rattling at the oven door. She opened it and, **to her surprise**, out jumped the little gingerbread man she had made. She tried to catch him as he ran across the kitchen, but **he slipped past her** and shouted, "Run, run, as fast as you can! You can't catch me; I'm the gingerbread man!" The ginger-bread man ran out into the garden where the old wom-an's husband tried **unsuccessfully** to catch him. The old couple tried to run after him, but he was too fast! A cow and a horse tried to stop the gingerbread man, but he was too quick for them, too. Finally, the gingerbread man came across a fox. Again he shouted, "Run, run, as fast as you can! You can't catch me; I'm the gingerbread man!" But, even though the sly fox was hungry, he sim-ply said, "Why would I bother trying to catch you?" Just after he had passed the fox, the gingerbread man had to stop when he came to a wide, deep river. The crafty fox came along and offered to carry the gingerbread man on his back across the river. When they were **halfway** across the fox said, "You are going to have to stand on my head, gingerbread man, or else **you'll get wet!**" The gingerbread man was happy to do so and the two con-tinued across the river. Then the fox said, "You're still getting a little wet on my head. Why don't you move to my nose?" The gingerbread man happily jumped onto the fox's nose, but when they reached the bank of the river the fox suddenly opened his mouth with a snap! The gingerbread man disappeared into the fox's mouth and **was never seen again.**

EL HOMBRE DE JENGIBRE

Un día una vieja estaba haciendo pan de jengibre. Con la masa sobrante creó **la figura** de un pequeño hombre. Utilizó caramelos rojos para los ojos, la nariz y la boca, y puso chocolatinas a lo largo del pecho a modo de botones. Después lo puso sobre papel de horno y lo metió en el **horno** para cocerlo. Pasado un tiempo oyó que algo golpeaba la puerta del horno. Y **cuál no fue su sorpresa** cuando, al abrirla, salió el pequeño hombre de jengibre que había creado. Lo persiguió por la cocina, pero él **se escurrió** y le gritó: «¡Corre, corre tan rápido como puedas! No puedes atraparme, ¡soy el hombre de jengibre!». El hombre de jengibre corrió hasta el jardín, donde el marido de la vieja intentó atraparlo **sin éxito**. La pareja de ancianos intentó correr tras él, pero ¡era demasiado rápido! Una vaca y un caballo intentaron de-tenerlo, pero también era demasiado rápido para ellos. Por último, el hombre de jengibre se encontró con un zorro. De nuevo gritó: «¡Corre, corre tan rápido como puedas! No puedes atraparme, ¡soy el hombre de jen-gibre!». Sin embargo, a pesar de que el astuto zorro estaba hambriento, le respondió: «¿Para qué me iba a molestar en intentar atraparte?». Nada más sobrepasar al zorro, el hombre de jengibre tuvo que detenerse ante un río ancho y profundo. El astuto zorro se acercó y se ofreció a llevarlo en su lomo hasta la otra orilla del río. **A mitad** del recorrido, el zorro le dijo: «Vas a tener que subirte a mi cabeza, hombre de jengibre, ¡o **te moja-rás**!». El hombre de jengibre se mostró encantado de hacerlo, y ambos continuaron su camino para cruzar el río. Entonces el zorro dijo: «Todavía te mojas un poco sobre mi cabeza, ¿por qué no te subes a mi nariz?». El hombre de jengibre así lo hizo, pero cuando alcanzaron la orilla del río, ¡el zorro abrió la boca de repente con un chasquido! El hombre de jengibre desapareció en la boca del zorro y **nunca más se le volvió a ver.**

THREE BILLY GOATS GRUFF

Once upon a time there were three billy goats, and all of them were called "Gruff." **They were hungry** so they decided to go up to the hillside to feed. They came upon a bridge, and **under** the bridge lived a great ugly troll. First of all came the youngest billy goat **to cross** the bridge. "Trip, trap, trip, trap!" went the bridge. "Who's that tripping over my bridge?" roared the troll. "It is only I, the tiniest billy goat Gruff," said the billy goat, with a small voice. "I'm coming to gobble you up," said the troll. "Oh, no! Please don't eat me. **I'm too little**," said the billy goat. "Wait a bit till the second billy goat Gruff comes. He's much bigger." "Well, **be off with you**," said the troll. A little while after came the second billy goat Gruff to cross the bridge. "Trip, trap, trip, trap," went the bridge. "Who's that tripping over my bridge?" roared the troll. "Oh, it's the second billy goat Gruff, and I'm going up to the hillside to make myself fat," said the billy goat. "Now I'm coming to gobble you up," said the troll. "Oh, no! Don't eat me. Wait a little until the big billy goat Gruff comes. He's much bigger." "Very well! Be off with you," said the troll. But just then up came the big billy goat Gruff. "Trip, trap, trip, trap, trip, trap!" went the bridge, for the billy goat was so heavy that the bridge groaned under him. "Who's that tramping over my bridge?" roared the troll. "It is me! The big billy goat Gruff," said the billy goat, who had an ugly hoarse voice of his own. "Now I'm coming to gobble you up," roared the troll. But the big billy goat Gruff **was not afraid**. He flew at the troll, and poked his eyes out with his **horns**, and crushed him to bits, body and **bones**, and tossed him out into the stream. After that he went up to the hillside with his brothers, and there the billy goats got so fat that they were scarcely able to walk home again.

TRES MACHOS CABRÍOS GRUFF

Había una vez tres machos cabríos, y a todos ellos los llamaban «Gruff». **Estaban hambrientos**, así que decidieron subir a la montaña a alimentarse. Llegaron a un puente, **debajo del** cual vivía un enorme y feo trol. Primero fue a **cruzar** el puente el macho cabrío más joven. «¡Trip, trap, trip, trap!», crujió el puente. «¿Quién camina sobre mi puente?», gruñó el trol. «Solo soy yo, el más pequeño macho cabrío Gruff», respondió el macho cabrío con un hilo de voz. «Voy a engullirte», le contestó el trol. «¡Oh, no! Por favor, no me comas, **soy demasiado pequeño** –replicó el macho cabrío–. Espera a que venga el segundo macho cabrío Gruff. Es mucho más grande». «Muy bien, pues **lárgate**», dijo el trol. Poco después llegó el segundo macho cabrío Gruff para cruzar el puente. «¡Trip, trap, trip, trap!», crujió el puente. «¿Quién camina sobre mi puente?», gruñó el trol. «Soy el segundo macho cabrío, voy a la montaña para engordar», contestó el macho cabrío. «Voy a engullirte», le advirtió el trol. «¡Oh, no! Por favor, no me comas –dijo el macho cabrío–. Espera a que venga el gran macho cabrío Gruff. Es mucho más grande». «Muy bien, adelante», replicó el trol. Y entonces llegó el macho cabrío Gruff mayor. «¡Trip, trap, trip, trap, trip, trap!», crujió el puente, pues el macho cabrío era tan enorme que el puente gemía bajo su peso. «¿Quién camina sobre mi puente?», gruño el trol. «¡Soy yo! El macho cabrío mayor», respondió el macho cabrío, que por su parte tenía una horrenda voz ronca. «Voy a devorarte», rugió el trol. Sin embargo, el macho cabrío mayor **no tenía miedo**. Se lanzó contra el trol, le sacó los ojos con su **cornamenta**; le dio tal paliza que hizo trizas su cuerpo entero, incluidos los **huesos**, y lo lanzó al torrente. Cuando hubo terminado subió a la montaña con sus hermanos, y tan gordos se pusieron que casi no podían caminar de regreso a casa.